Ogres Don't Like Lemons!

Michael Greene

c/b

DeBokton Book

DeBokton.weebly.com

ISBN-13:978-1985652729

ISBN-10:1985652722

Chapters

This book is dedicated and all the parents who want to scream when they are reading chapter books with their children. May you find this as fun to read as your children enjoy reading or hearing it.

Chapter 1: The Unusual Interview

Peter walked into the office of Woodcreek Academy. It didn't seem like a normal school, there were pictures of dragons and vampires on the wall. Why would someone fill the minds of children with such frivolous creatures? Although, he needed a

job, and this was the only school that taught Latin in the area.

The lady at the desk called him and told him, "Peter, Irlore will see you now."

He went in and asked the kid at the desk, "Where's the headmaster?"

The kid clasped his hands together, jumped into the seat at the desk and said, "I'm Irlore, the headmaster. I'm much older than I look. Would you like a cookie?"

Peter looked at him oddly and said, "I'm here about the job as a Latin teacher. I am very..."

"Yes yes, you're hired. Now are you good with students with special needs?"

"Yes."

"OK. What would you do if one of the students tries to eat one of the other students?"

Peter stared at him, "What?"

"Oh, don't worry, you'll learn. Do you carry a weapon?"

"No."

"You probably should, you'll find some in the teachers lounge. Whatever you want. You are human, aren't you?"

"Yes."

Irlore leaned a little closer and said, "Do you realize the risk of that? Try to stay away from the west wing at night. I hope you know magic."

Peter looked at him oddly, "You can't be the headmaster, where is he?"

Irlore thought for a moment, "Okay." Irlore went out and came back in, "Hi! I'm Headmaster Irlore. You have the job. Have fun! My secretary will give you all the details."

"Wait, I haven't decided to work here. This place is still very odd, and my family will have to move for this."

"Of course you want the job. Did I tell you that it pays over three times that of a normal teacher's pay?"

"I'm listening."

"Talk to my Secretary for now. Bye." Headmaster Irlore brought Peter to his Secretary, she introduced herself as Frieda. Irlore said, "OK, they're having a dance tonight, and I have to make sure the sprites don't get duct taped to the wall as decorations."

Irlore left, and Peter wondered why someone would duct tape soda to the wall? He looked at Frieda and said, "So, you're giving me a tour?"

"Yes, let's start." She said with a nice smile, "Follow me." She started doing cartwheels down the hall. Peter just walked like a normal person. After a while, Frieda stopped and turned left, "This is the cafeteria. You should eat over there." She stated.

He looked at her, "Why?"

"You might taste good with ketchup. Anyway, we have everything in here that you might eat. We have food for the herbivores, food for the carnivores, food for the omnivores, and a blood bank over there."

Peter asked, "Why do you have a blood bank?"

Frieda looked at him with a confused look "Would you want to be without one? Lets go." As they walked to the gymnasium, Peter was confused about why Frieda was doing cartwheels and backhand springs down the hall. *This school is definitely weird*, he thought. Frieda stopped and said, "You might

want to let me in first. I don't want to scare you too much on your first day." She opened the door and called in, "Everyone, get down, act human!"

"Act human?" Peter asked.

Frieda looked at him and said, "Would you rather they act like animals?" They stepped in, and there were lots of kids staring at him. It was odd. They weren't a normal group of kids. They dressed very oddly, looked tough, and Peter thought that the seven foot tall hairy guy might want to eat him. Peter thought one of them coughed fire, but Frieda rushed him away too quickly for him

to be sure. He must have been imagining things.

As they hurried away from the gym. He literally ran into someone in the hall. Frieda did a dive-roll over him, so she didn't fall over. The boy held out his hand, "I'm Vladimir. It's nice to meet you. You smell very good. A positive?"

Peter stared at him oddly, "What?"

"Don't worry about it." Vladimir said. "I've gotta go now. See ya." He walked down the hall to a door and went in.

Peter felt in a daze throughout the whole tour. He didn't understand why they named the wings of the school that the boarding students stayed in after mythical creatures, like the vampire wing and pixie wing, but it paid well, and the students seemed nice enough, so he took the job.

Frieda told him, "One of the perks of the job is free tuition, if your children are clever enough to come to school here."

Peter assured her that his kids were very smart. Hopefully they would like this school.

He then heard a loud shriek and a roar from outside the building. "What was that?" he asked.

"Nothing important," Frieda assured him. Then she added, "But I do suggest that you get a weapon from the teacher's lounge."

Chapter 2: The First Day of School

Peter's children, Daniel, James, and Sue, walked into Woodcreek Academy on the first day of school. They had just moved to their new house so they didn't know anyone there. They all stopped and stared at the students in the hallway. Sue, who was only eight, tugged at her oldest brother's arm.

She pointed at a boy, "Is he human?" She asked.

Daniel eyed him cautiously. "I'm sure he is, but he does look rather troll-like."

His thirteen year old brother, James, leaned over to him, pointing at another student and asked, "Why does that boy have fangs? The probability of such an oddity is a rare event." He then looked at another student and asked, "Were we supposed to dress up, or is that kid's tail real?"

Daniel shrugged, "I don't know, but it looks like this is going to be an interesting school year." Daniel made sure his siblings got to their classes, and then went to his first class, which he thought would be pre-calculus, since he was a junior. He was surprised when he saw the books on the desk said *The Mathematics of Dimensional Anomalies*.

The students started coming in and one sat in the seat next to his. She had very dark hair and very light skin. She looked at him and said, "Hi, I'm Velvet. You're new here."

He looked at her with a confused look. "What's up with this school? Is the first day of school costume day?"

Velvet laughed at him. "What's so funny?" Daniel asked.

Velvet looked like she was holding back a laugh when she said, "You don't know? You seriously don't know?"

"Don't know what?" he asked.

She was laughing as she said, "This school is for non-humans. You are allowed here, but only about five percent of the people

here are human." she explained. "Oh, you're going to be in for lots of surprises."

He smiled and said, "OK, I'll play along. What kind of creature are you?"

"A vampire."Velvet answered.

"If you're a vampire, shouldn't you be sleeping in a coffin, and trying to drink my blood?"

Velvet simply said, "Vampires aren't undead, they are just another species that needs to drink blood to survive, and I only eat

blood at the blood bank. Besides, I'm not hungry."

He thought that was an interesting form of vampire. "So how about sunlight? Does it kill you?"

"Of course not." Velvet answered, "We just don't tan, so we burn easily. Plus, we have enhanced eyesight, so we're more sensitive to sunlight."

Daniel smiled, "My brother's going to love this. How does sunlight affect trolls? Do they really turn to stone? Or is that another legend?"

"They harden in the sunlight and it drains the color out of their skin; but they thaw when the sun goes down. The light doesn't kill them." Then she added, "It's also fun to draw a mustache on them when they're frozen."

"Do dragons exist?"

"Of course they do."

"I knew it! And everyone called me a nerd." Daniel explained with an excited look on his face. "How big are they?"

"They're as big as a cat, or as big as a horse."

"Thanks Velvet, this school is going to be awesome. No one at my old school had any imagination. And you came in here pretending to be a vampire."

Velvet would have said something, but she was interrupted by the teacher calling the class to start. She was very short, probably only 4 and a half feet tall, had blue hair, and wore a sparkly cape; not what you'd expect from a math teacher.

"Before we get started, we have a new student. Daniel, can you stand?" Daniel stood, then the teacher informed them, "He's 16, a straight A student, and our token human. Don't worry, no one will hold that against you."

Daniel didn't understand, was the whole school playing a trick on him? He wanted to know, but first he had to get through class.

The teacher said that they where going to talk about important numbers. Daniel thought she would talk about numbers like pi, e, and phi, but instead she spoke of how many times you have to run around a fairy ring to enter it

safely, lunar cycles and how they effect werewolves, and magic. It sounds simple, but dimensional anomalies are hard to work with. The math is very complicated. Daniel thought he was good at math, but he'd never heard of a topological space before, but the other kids seemed to know about it quite well. This school was going to challenge him.

When class was finished, Daniel looked at his schedule. His next class was *Wizardry for Humans* with headmaster Irlore as the teacher. He seriously thought that these people where trying to mess with his head.

He went to that classroom. It wasn't a large class, but everyone in it looked human; and to his surprise, his thirteen year old brother and eight year old sister were in it as well. How many classrooms had an eight year old a thirteen year old and a sixteen year old?

Irlore came in, "Hello children. Now who wants to learn some magic!?!

Chapter 3: The Lesson in Magic

Irlore was standing in front of the class when he said, "For those of you that haven't attended this class. Magic is a substance from another dimension that reacts to sound in unusual ways, like making a fireball, or sending you into someones mind." He jumped and didn't fall back down, he just floated.

"This is a demonstration. Does anyone have any questions?"

Daniel raised his hand, "How did you do that?"

"With magic, my dear boy. Does anyone have any questions that aren't obvious?"

James raised his hand, "How do you access another dimension?"

"With a magical artifact." Irlore said floating upside down, "It doesn't matter what type of magical artifact it is, any will allow

you to access the dimension of magic. Any other..."

"Do you have a unicorn?" Sue almost screamed.

"Frieda does.

"If there are no more questions, we'll move on to spells." Irlore gave them all a piece of paper and all except Sue a wand, "Memorize these words. I'm going to run though the wall." He did.

Daniel was excited about seeing what the people who had been using magic for years

could do. He was disappointed when the best any of them could do is light a small fire. He decided to give it a try, "Cloro-ferno!" Nothing happened. "Clormo-ferno!" A small puff of smoke appeared.

One of the other students came over, "How did you do that?"

"I'm sorry?"

"It took me months to learn to do that, and you learned that in just two tries!"

"Are you saying that I'm a natural wizard?"

"Yes! At this rate, you'll be an omega level wizard in months. Oh, I'm Andrew." He held out his hand, "What's your name?"

"Daniel." Daniel answered. He looked at his wand, "Clorma-ferno!" This time there was a very small fireball. "This is amazing! She wasn't lying! Dragons do exist!!!"

Andrew looked at him and said, "What?"

Irlore came in with some odd items, "Daniel, James, spiky hair, and stinky come here."

"For the last time, my name is Robert." spiky hair scolded.

"And my name's Samuel!" stinky complained.

"Whatever you say, spiky hair and stinky." Irlore started laughing at himself. He showed them all of the the items he had, "This is a magical item, you can draw magic from it. Choose one." They all did. Sue raised her hand. "Yes unicorn?"

"Why didn't I get a magical item?"

"Because you're not ready for it my child. At your age you try to learn how to pronounce the words." He patted her head, then went to Daniel. Irlore gave Daniel a ring. It was a black ring, with a shining metallic blue band around it, and a single red gem inset at the front. "You should use this. You have more potential than anyone else here. Just like I did, I was awesome."

Daniel was about to say he made his choice on a magical item, but it was in Irlore's other hand. "How did you take my amulet?"

"Do I have to answer?"

Daniel nodded, "Right, magic." He then thought for a moment. "You said you need a magical artifact and to say magic words to cast a spell. You don't say any words, and I don't see an artifact on you. How do you do it?"

"This was mine. Use it well." Irlore said with a serious look on his face

That was the first time Daniel saw him stop smiling. He put the ring on. It felt strong. "Clorma-ferno!" The fireball appeared in his hand. It wasn't big and it didn't last long, but it was bigger than his last one. "Why do you want me to have this?"

"I'll tell you in a bit." He assured him, "Go have fun." He jumped on the ceiling and started tap-dancing.

Sue was staring in awe, Daniel was looking at him wondering why he did the things he did, James was trying to figure out how much wind pressure would be needed to do that, and one of the students said, "Just another Tuesday."

After the lesson was over, Irlore told them that there was a dance tonight and that they should come.

Sue walked up to Irlore, "Can I have a unicorn?"

"I'll talk to Frieda." Irlore assured her.

Sue walked up to Daniel, "I'm getting a unicorn!!!" She screamed with excitement. "That's much better than a pony."

Daniel smiled, "I can't wait." He walked out of the classroom and straight to Velvet. "Velvet, can you tell me more about this school?"

"Sure, what do you want to know?" She said with a smile on her face. "Did you do well in class?"

"I made a small fireball." Daniel explained.

"On your first day?" She exclaimed, "Can you do it again?"

"OK." He held out his hand, "Clorma-ferno!" Like before there was a small fireball.

She looked even more excited, "You may be the second most powerful wizard soon!"

Chapter 4: The Bully

Daniel and Velvet went into the cafeteria. Daniel pulled out his lunch, Velvet went to the blood bank. When she came back, she had a werewolf and a fairy with her.

Velvet sat down. "They have AB negative today. Want some? ... No you don't."

The fairy came over, "Who is this? Is he your boyfriend?" She asked Velvet.

Daniel wasn't sure what to say.

Velvet just rolled her eyes, "No, we just met today."

"Oh, in that case." She flew over to him. "I'm Blossom, and I'm single."

Velvet hit her. "I'm sorry, but you know how fairies are. Well, maybe you don't, but they're big flirts."

Blossom started poking him. "So you really are a human."

The werewolf smelled him, "Yes, he's a human. I'm Conner."

"I'm Daniel." He said, obviously scared.

"You're freaked out because I'm a wolf, aren't you?" Conner stated as if it happened all the time.

"Kind of." Daniel answered.

Blossom then went over to Velvet, "What's kissing a human like?"

Velvet face-palmed, "We aren't dating."

Blossom smiled and asked Daniel, "Can I find out what kissing a human is like?"

"No." Daniel answered instantly.

Blossom then looked at Conner. "That's a very balanced diet." She said with a sarcastic voice.

Conner had a large steak with a side dish of bacon and wings. He then pointed at a slice of pickle, "I have my vegetable."

Blossom would have said more, but an ogre bumped into Daniel, "Oh, sorry. Didn't see you there." The way he said that sounded

like he did it on purpose. "Human, what are you doing at this school?"

"Having lunch." Daniel replied with a straight face.

The ogre looked mad when he said, "No, what are you doing here, human?"

"Just having lunch, but I like it that you care that much about me." Daniel said having fun mocking him.

"Humans are worthless and shouldn't be in charge." he almost yelled.

A mummy walked by. "I think you're all worthless," he mocked as he did.

The ogre grabbed Daniel and said, "You'll regret coming to this school."

Daniel cocked his head, "Does that mean you don't want my autograph?" He started laughing at himself.

The ogre threw him back into his seat. "You'll fear the name of Brock." He walked off.

"Who's that guy?" Daniel asked Velvet.

"Brock, he really doesn't like humans." Velvet answered.

Blossom frowned, "Why didn't you ask me? Are you two in love or something?"

"For the last time, we aren't dating." Velvet informed her.

Daniel looked at Blossom. She was bigger than a traditional fairy, she was about three feet tall. He then asked, "Blossom, what are fairies like?"

"What?"

"What are fairies really like compared to fantasy?" Daniel explained.

"Well, we have leathered flight. We're bigger, obviously." Blossom batted her eyes, "And much prettier, don't you think?"

Daniel shook his head. "Seriously," he muttered. "You have leathered flight, like bat wings? You look more like you have insect wings."

She smiled. "Look closer." She put her wing right in his face so he couldn't see a thing.

Velvet grabbed her shirt and pulled her back. "Sorry about her," she apologized to Daniel. "Don't worry; not all fairies are like her. Some are only horrible pranksters who you want to duct tape to the wall."

Daniel eyed her. "Are we actually allowed to do that here? I mean, in this school, I have to ask."

"No," Velvet answered. "But it is tempting."

Daniel then turned to Conner. "How do werewolves work?"

"We go through a metamorphosis," Conner explained. "We look pretty human as babies, except we have claws and facial hair. Then as we get older, we change, kind of like a butterfly. The transformation doesn't take long." He then posed. "It's a good look on me, isn't it?"

"If you like really hairy guys, I guess so," Velvet responded. "Personally, I think you need a shave." She then changed the subject and suggested, "Let's go watch the Gorffelball game."

"Gorffelball?" Daniel asked.

"Sure, come watch," Velvet suggested. As they walked out of the cafeteria, she explained. "Gorffelball is kind of like basketball, but with no rules, and it doesn't have baskets, it has hoops. It doesn't use a basketball either. And there are no fouls, unless you seriously injure or kill someone. Then you are expelled from the school and turned over to the police. But, other than that, it's just like basketball."

That didn't sound like basketball at all to Daniel. "Can the police actually hold non-humans in jail?"

"It depends on the race," Velvet answered. "If the police can't handle a race, Irlore turns the criminal into a frog and puts him in detention. There are a few criminals who will be frogs for life. Fortunately, Irlore is nice to his pets."

Velvet also explained that lunch was long, because some races needed to eat large amounts of food to keep them from eating their classmates. The students, who didn't have to eat as long, often played a Gorffelball game at lunch.

Daniel watched the game. It reminded him of two toddlers fighting over a ball, except there were twenty of them, with fangs, claws, wings, and magic. The giant playing had a huge advantage, and there was a humanoid tree. Daniel had never seen anything like it.

Brock walked over and shoved Daniel's shoulder. "You should get on the field, so I can get on and kill you."

"I'm not scared of you," Daniel responded.

"You should be," Brock threatened. "Go home!" He then went on the field, threw a leprechaun off of it so he could take his place, and started pounding anyone he could, pretending to go for the ball.

A half-dragon accidentally set the tree on fire. Irlore was watching the game, so he put it out quickly enough so no real damage was done. Still, the half-dragon got sent to detention for the afternoon.

Velvet had seen plenty Gorffelball games, so she turned to Daniel. "You are coming to the dance tonight, aren't you?"

"I guess so," Daniel answered. "I hadn't thought much about it."

Blossom flew over to him. "I'll be your date to the dance."

"No, Blossom," Velvet answered for Daniel. "He needs to get to meet people tonight." She then asked Daniel, "Can you dance?"

"I can sway to the music," Daniel answered. He then cautiously asked, "What should I expect? I assume this won't be a normal school dance."

"It will be normal, well… for us." She shrugged. "With Irlore in charge, anything is normal for him."

They watched the game a while longer. As they started to leave, Brock bumped into him. "Go home, human!" Brock threatened. "Don't even think about going to the dance tonight. I'll cream you."

Chapter 5: Dinner at Home

Peter and his family were having dinner when Peter asked Daniel, "How was school today, son?"

"I met a Vampire named Velvet, a Werewolf named Conner, and an annoying little fairy named Blossom. I also learned magic." Daniel answered.

Peter fake laughed, "OK, very funny. What was school really like?"

"Just liked I answered," Daniel responded.

Peter looked at James. "James, you might be more likely to not make up an answer. What happened at school?"

James answered with, "I learned about a substance that reacts to sound."

Peter looked interested, "Really, what's it called?"

"The man that told us about it called it magic." James answered. "Daniel learned the sound to make a fireball with it."

"James, I think you've spent too much time with Daniel. You're getting his personality. Magic doesn't exist, and never will," Peter scolded.

"Yes it does," Daniel explained. "This school is full of magic, and monsters and fae, and really weird teachers."

Peter looked at Sue, "Tell me what happened, don't make anything up."

"Irlore told me he'd get me a unicorn!" She said with excitement.

Peter raised his voice at Daniel. "Stop filling their minds with fantasy!"

"I didn't, they saw it for themselves." Daniel insisted, "I can prove that we're telling the truth."

"No! Stop lying!" Peter yelled, "If there were real monsters in this school or that they were teaching you magic, I'd pull you out in a heartbeat!"

Daniel took a deep breath, "It was a normal day for this school."

James started saying "Normal for this school is..." Daniel elbowed him. "What was that for?"

Daniel whispered to James, "We want to stay here." Daniel told his Dad, "I went to math, met a few friends, and I'm going to the dance. You're not going, right?"

"No." Peter answered, "Why?"

"Good, I mean, no reason." Daniel answered.

Daniel ate his dinner very quietly so as not to concern his father. They all listened to Sue talking about unicorns. That didn't make Daniel's Dad think that there were non-human creatures at the school, because Sue talked about unicorns all the time. After a while, Peter went out to put some oil in the car. The kids started to help their mother clean up dinner.

"There really are non-humans at the school." Daniel explained.

His mother looked at him and smiled, "Of course there are. Why do you think I told your father to go there? How would I even

know about Woodcreek Academy if I never went there?"

James looked shocked. "Are you a non-human, or do you know magic? If you are non-human, than that would mean that I'm only half human."

"I'm human," Their mother answered. "But I did learn some magic. Although, I forgot most of it."

"Why haven't you told us until now?" Daniel asked.

"Well, your Dad doesn't know I went there, or like the idea of magic, or me telling you magic's real." She answered. "If you want, I can grab my wand. There's a reason I make good ice cream. Ice magic was my specialty."

Daniel answered, "Of course we want to see some magic!"

She went upstairs and got a wand. "I'm back. Glacio!" She made a ball of ice. "Want some? It tastes very good. My ice is flavored. What do you think the secret to my smoothies is? Don't tell your Dad."

Daniel got excited, "Is that why I'm gifted in magic?"

"What do you mean?" She asked.

Daniel held out his hand, "Clorma-ferno!" There was a fireball in his hand.

Their mom jumped back. "You learned that in a day?"

"Yes, Velvet said I might be the second most powerful wizard soon." Daniel answered.

Their mom was about to say something when Peter came in. "Kim, do you have a fire extinguisher?"

"It's by the door." Kim answered, "Is something wrong?"

"Nothing major. I could just use a fire extinguisher." Peter answered. He got the fire extinguisher. As he went out he called, "I'm going to the store to pick up some more oil."

Kim then told Daniel and James, "You should go to the dance now, but before you do, remember, don't encourage the fairies, they're big enough flirts already. Don't let a

vampire bite you. Don't make a troll laugh, they spit all over the place when they do; and ogres hate lemons. I found that useful. Now, you better get going.

Chapter 6: The Zero-Gravity Dance

Daniel and James walked into the ballroom. They were wearing polo shirts and slacks. They hoped that was good enough dress. When they went in, people were wearing everything from shorts to tuxedos. They noticed that there was tons of food, and that the decorations had lots of sparkles. Irlore

wasn't in sight, and there wasn't music. "Why isn't there music?" Daniel asked.

Velvet came over. "Hi. You're just in time." She pulled him and his brother James, into the crowd, and looked at the stage at the end of the room.

There was a puff of smoke and Irlore appeared. "Hello everyone! Now, I'm guessing you want to know what the theme of this dance is." They roared in approval. "Well, the theme is..." he snapped and music started playing. "Levitation!!!" He stomped and everyone started floating in the air. Irlore did a quadruple back flip and started flying.

Daniel asked Velvet, "How are we supposed to dance without gravity?"

"Irlore lets us figure that out ourselves," Velvet answered.

James looked like he was thinking about something. "This music sounds like a cross between fairy music and howling."

Irlore told everyone to get a partner and start dancing.

Several Fairies tried to dance with Daniel. He didn't dance with any of them. Instead he asked Velvet to dance.

After a while, Velvet asked Daniel, "Want to meet some of the vampires?"

"Sure, what's the worst that could happen?" Daniel answered.

Velvet considered it. "Well, you could die, but not likely," she assured him. "Plus they brought pizza. Don't eat it."

On their way a small man with red hair swam through the air by them. "Hi, I'm Taylor." He said. Then swam off.

"What was he?" Daniel asked Velvet.

"A sprite," she answered. They swam to the vampires eating pizza. "Daniel, this is the vampire crowd: Vladimir, Victor, Vicki, Valerie, and Hubert."

"Hubert's name stands out," Daniel noted.

Vladimir floated over. "So, you're Daniel, the natural sorcerer Velvet keeps speaking of." He shook his hand. "Are the stories Velvet tells about you real?"

"What stories?" Daniel asked.

Velvet looked embarrassed. "I told them about how you learned a spell in a day," she admitted.

"Dude, that's awesome," Vladimir replied. "We should hangout at my place. We'll bring human pizza." He stopped, realizing what he said. "That is, pizza made for humans, not pizza made of... You get the idea."

Velvet chuckled.

A blue haired sprite floated by, "Hi, I'm Taylor." Then proceeded to say the same thing to each individual Vampire.

Daniel looked confused. "Wasn't the last sprite named Taylor?"

"Yes," Velvet answered. "It's confusing." Then Velvet suggested, "Let's get back to dancing. You asked me." They started dancing again. After awhile, they danced over the tree man that caught on fire at the Gorffelball game. He was standing on the ground talking to a tree girl who was floating upside-down.

"Why isn't he floating?" Daniel asked.

"That's Rowan." Velvet answered. "He's immune to magic."

"Then how come he caught on fire at the Gorffelball game?" Daniel asked.

"He isn't immune to fire, but he's immune to spells cast on him." She told him.

They danced a little bit longer, before Daniel spun her around, and they accidentally ran into a Giant. She was about eight feet tall. "Sorry," Velvet apologized. "I didn't see you there."

The Giant girl looked at her with no expression. Then she smiled and said, "Don't worry, it happens all the time." Then she looked at Daniel. "You're the new kid. I'm

Teeny, and this is my friend Steven." He was about a foot taller than her.

Daniel looked at her. *Teeny?* he thought. She's bigger than me. He asked Velvet, "Why's her name Teeny?"

Velvet giggled, "Because she's small for a Giant. Giants are usually nine feet tall."

A pink haired sprite came over. "Hi, I'm..."

"Let me guess, Taylor?" Daniel asked.

The sprite looked confused. "No, I'm Erland Jackson Scott Michael Todd Elijah

Jones the three-hundredth and ninety-third. Just kidding, I'm Taylor." He laughed and swam off through the air.

Daniel and Velvet went back to dancing. When the song was over, they all floated carefully back down to the floor, except for James, who had been experimenting with the zero gravity punch, and spilled his punch all over himself, and Drake, who was half dragon, and came down hard enough to crack the floor, and Brock, who... Well, they didn't all float down carefully.

Brock was purposely clinging to the rafters of the ceiling. He made his way to the

disco ball hanging from the center, which was right over Daniel, and knocked it down.

Conner, the werewolf, made a great dive over Daniel and caught it. He looked at it casually, and threw it to Irlore, calling, "Catch!" as he threw.

Irlore levitated it back up to the middle of the ceiling, and scolded Brock, "That's my fourth favorite disco ball. Don't break it!" He then levitated him down to the floor and warned, "Watch it! You'd look very good as a frog."

Brock stormed over to the other side of the room, as he did, he bumped into Daniel and sneered, "You will regret coming here."

"I don't think so," Daniel replied calmly. "I'm not afraid of you." He pulled three small lemons from his pocket and started juggling them.

Brock backed away and covered his nose. "You stink!" Then he warned, "You should be afraid of me," but his threat wasn't bold, as he seemed to be reacting as if he'd just taken a whiff of hot pepper. He hurried away, and went over to five other ogres and

said something, but Daniel couldn't hear what he said.

Daniel put the lemons on the food table he'd picked them up from. "I guess ogres don't like lemons," he noted.

"Not as much as they don't like humans," Velvet teased.

Daniel looked back over at the ogres who were still talking about something, likely him.

A minute later, the ogres walked out of the room. Daniel looked over at Velvet and

asked, "Should we follow them? I have a bad feeling about that guy."

"I'm with you," Velvet responded.

Blossom then responded, "I'm coming too." He hadn't even been aware that she was around until she spoke.

Daniel sighed. "No, Blossom, please don't come. We'll attract enough attention with two of us."

"I can help," Blossom defended. "I don't have magic, but I do have fairy sparkles."

"Um… That will make us more obvious," Daniel pointed out.

"My sparkles can help us blend in to the surroundings," Blossom explained. "You really don't know your way around this school, do you?"

"Fine," Daniel conceded. "We have to hurry, or we'll lose them."

"Not likely," Blossom stated happily. "Fairies are really good trackers. Follow me!" She then flew off in front of them.

They found Brock and the other ogres in the courtyard.

"I hope your sparkles can hide us," Daniel whispered as they all hid behind a bench. It was the only thing near enough to hear.

"We need to get Daniel out of here!" Brock was ranting. "He is not afraid of us as most humans are."

"I hear he has strong magic too," Butch, one of the other ogres, warned. "He isn't going to be controllable."

A smaller ogre named Sam then asked, "Why do we want to control the humans anyway? They're harmless."

"They're not! If Daniel stays here too long, he'll learn more magic," Brock almost yelled. "Humans and ogres have never gotten along. They are the enemy!"

Sam shrugged, "Maybe it's time to change that."

"No!" Brock yelled. "If you suggest that again, I'll feed you to the dragon."

"But the dragon's a vegetar..." Sam started to say, but then thought better of it and got suddenly quiet.

Brock continued, "We can't scare Daniel away, but we can scare his father away. If his father goes, he'll go too."

"Good plan," Butch agreed. "How do we scare him off?"

"We'll catch him," Brock explained. "Then we'll reveal that we aren't human. If that doesn't scare him off, a little pain will. I enjoy fighting humans."

Daniel almost gasped, but instead clenched the bench to keep himself from making a sound and getting them discovered.

"We'll put the plan in action the night after tomorrow," Brock instructed.

"Um… what plan?" Chad, another of the ogres asked. "All I got was we capture him. Did I miss the details?"

Brock thought for a moment. "We'll write a note to him, asking for help with our Latin homework tomorrow night. Then when he comes to meet with us, we'll jump him,

put a bag over his head, and take him to the pit. That will scare him away."

Sam timidly pointed out, "We aren't taking Latin, and..." Brock glared at him, so Sam apologized. "I am sorry, Brock. I do not wish to be fed to the vegetarian dragon."

The group of ogres then walked off.

"What do we do?" Daniel asked. "They're going after my father!"

"You'll come up with something," Blossom assured him. "You're really smart,

and really handsome too. We should go dance."

They did all go back to the dance. Everyone was floating around again, and there were things that looked like huge marshmallows floating around with them. They were randomly exploding into shimmering butterflies. It definitely was going to be an interesting night.

Chapter 7: The Vampire Cave

After dinner the next night, Daniel drove back to Woodcreek Academy. Many of the students lived at the school, but Daniel's family lived a few minutes drive from it.

He parked his car and started walking to the vampire cave when he was stopped by Irlore. It seemed more than coincidence.

Irlore skipped over to him and happily said, "Daniel, it's good to see you." Then he got serious and added, "Don't let Brock scare you. You are destined for great things. You have strong magic. Why do you think I was so eager to hire your dad? I wanted you at this school. There will come a day where its survival will depend on you." He then shook his head. "Ok, enough serious business. I'm going to go make chocolate chip, spinach cookies. Have fun with Velvet." He then

sprang away, saying, "Boing, boing, bunny, boing boing,..."

Daniel wondered what Irlore meant by *The survival of the school would depend on him,* but he also wasn't sure he should take what Irlore said too seriously. He continued on his way until he reached the vampire's cave.

The vampire's cave wasn't really a cave. The school wasn't by a mountain. It was just a building made to look like a cave.

He opened the door to the building, and bats flew out. Daniel ducked. When the bats

had passed, he looked around. The cave seemed to have many different caves in the walls of the main cave. There were bats hanging from stalactites that hung from the ceiling.

Daniel looked around, hoping to be able to find Velvet's cave, but Velvet was waiting for him. She came over. "There you are," she greeted. "Come on. Blossom and Conner are waiting."

She took him up to her cave, and pulled a statue of a pink bat to open her door.

When Daniel stepped in her cave, he was surprised to see that she had decorated in pink. Other than that, it looked pretty normal, except bigger than the average dorm room, and much darker. The only lighting was candles on a wall. There were no windows. Conner and Blossom were waiting.

They all sat around a very normal looking table, except it had a dagger stabbed in the middle of it as a centerpiece.

"What's the plan?" Velvet asked.

"I don't know," Daniel answered. "What resources do we have? All I can do is make a

small fireball." He thought for a moment. "Maybe I could learn an ice ball, but I think we are going to have to think our way out of this one. We'll need to outsmart Brock."

Blossom laughed. "Outsmarting him shouldn't be too hard. He's kind of dumb."

"He is dumb," Daniel agreed. "But he's really strong. We are going to have to be smart about this."

Conner suggested, "We can try to show Irlore that he's trying to kidnap your father. Irlore would probably turn Brock into a frog."

"We could," Daniel agreed, "But Brock will just come after us again. We need to show him that he can't mess with us."

Velvet suggested, "It will be dark tomorrow night. We might be able to make him think you are your dad."

"That's a good idea," Daniel agreed. "I really don't want my dad knowing this school's secret. He'd pull me out for sure."

"What secret?" Blossom asked.

"Most people don't know this is a school for non-humans," Daniel explained. "My dad doesn't know it."

"People in this city know," Blossom informed him.

Daniel continued with the plan. "We'll have to find a way for me to escape. I really don't want to die. Brock will be really angry when he finds out we've tricked him." He then asked Velvet, "How do lemons affect ogres?"

"Not too badly," Velvet explained. "They just don't like the smell, similar to how

vampires don't like the smell of garlic." She shuddered as she said it. "It's a horrible scent. Why would anyone like Italian food?"

Daniel scratched his head. "Weren't your vampire friends having pizza before?"

"Not pizza with garlic," she explained. "That wasn't tomato sauce on the pizza."

"Okay," Daniel responded, as he made a note never to eat vampire pizza. He then thought for a moment. "I have an idea!"

Chapter 8: Just Another Day at School

At breakfast the next morning. Peter told his family, "This school is nothing like any I've ever taught at. For the first day of classes, everyone was dressed up. They call the dorms after mythical creatures. The mascot is a dragon. I think they're obsessed with fantasy.

I'd have nothing to do with it, but the job pays very well."

"I like the school," Daniel assured him.

"I do too," James added.

"The students seem really odd," Peter explained. "I got a note from some students asking me to help them with their Latin tonight at 9:00 pm at my classroom."

"What's so odd about that?" Daniel asked.

Peter looked over at him and explained. "It's late. There is a tutoring lab, and oddest of all, the students aren't in my Latin class."

"Is there another Latin class?" Kim asked.

"No," Peter answered. "I'm the only Latin teacher."

"Who was it signed by?" Daniel asked. "Brock?"

His dad pulled the note out of his pocket and unfolded it. He looked at the bottom of

the page and answered, "Brock, Butch, Chad, David, Drew, and Sam."

"None of them are in your class?" Kim asked.

"No," Peter answered.

"Those guys are pranksters," Daniel explained. "Seriously, they are real ogres," he teased. "Just ignore the message."

"I probably will," his dad responded. "You know I'm not a night person. I'm not tutoring that late."

Daniel smiled. Keeping his dad away from the trap was going to be easier than he thought.

After breakfast, Peter went to the school to teach. After he left, Kim gave Daniel, James, and Sue the usual advice for kids from their mother before going to school. "Drive safely, don't forget your lunch, don't eat vampire pizza, and don't play chess with a sprite, they cheat."

He did drive safely. The day went pretty normally. At least normal for this school. On his way to gym class, a sprite walked by him. Daniel waved and said, "Hi Taylor."

The sprite jumped back. "How did you know my name?"

Daniel laughed. "Doesn't everyone?"

The sprite thought for a moment. "I am pretty popular."

Daniel went to gym class. The day was normal so far, but this wasn't normal. They were playing gorffelball, and Brock was in his gym class.

The gym coach told everyone that they were playing Gorffelball, and split everyone into teams.

Brock hissed at Daniel, "You're so dead!"

"We're on the same team." Daniel told him.

"I don't care!" Brock yelled. "I'm going to destroy your soul." He then looked over at the mummy in the class and mocked Daniel, "You'll end up just like him."

Velvet informed Daniel, "You should probably pass the ball as quickly as you can."

The coach blew the whistle. The ball fell from the air, and a Gargoyle flew up and

caught it before it hit the ground. Daniel looked at his opponents. They were intimidating, there was the gargoyle that caught the ball, a few goblins, a troll, Stephen the giant, a half-dragon, a minotaur, and Rowan. He was used to playing sports, but not used to opponents that could fly.

Brock ran straight for Daniel. Daniel didn't even notice, since the minotaur with the ball was headed straight for him. He then thought, "Why should I risk my life for one lousy point?" He looked back, and got an idea. He jumped out of the way, and the minotaur slammed into Brock, dropping the ball. Daniel grabbed the ball, "Thanks

Brock!" Then heeding Velvet's advice, he passed the ball quickly to Velvet.

Velvet caught the ball, pushed back the troll, ran quickly around Stephen the giant, pitched the ball to Conner, and tackled the gargoyle, who was about to tackle Conner, and Conner slammed the ball through the hoop.

Daniel was amazed at Velvet's skill; then he went flying as Brock kicked him across the court. It hurt. But Daniel noticed the ball flying towards him, so he grabbed it and threw it to Conner. "Thanks Brock, that was a good play!" he said.

The game went on pretty much like that. Brock kept trying to beat him up, but Daniel kept using it to his advantage.

After the game was over, Velvet told Daniel, "Good job! You survived your first Gorffelball game without us calling an ambulance! You don't even look hurt!"

"Trust me, some of those hits did hurt, but I wasn't going to let Brock have the satisfaction of knowing it. That's not how you deal with a bully."

They would have talked more, but then he saw Brock picking on a human girl.

He walked over and stood between Brock and the girl and said, "Brock, you don't need to show us you're a jerk! We already know!"

"Back off! I could beat you up right now!" Brock threatened.

"Oooh! So tough! You can beat up a human!" Daniel scratched his head, "Don't you think humans are an inferior race?"

"That's because you are! You could be beaten by a pixie!" Brock yelled.

"So does that mean you are as strong as a pixie?" Daniel asked.

"No! I'm stronger!" Brock countered.

"Then why are you trying to beat up a girl?" Daniel asked. "If you are as strong as you say, you shouldn't be having to prove anything.

"So how does beating up a girl that's half your height, an eighth of your weight, and at least 5 times your IQ prove you're strong?"

"I was showing her what her place is. She's human too! I'll prove my strength on you!" Brock boasted.

"So you were warming up on a girl? Aren't you afraid she would beat you up? After all, you're only as strong as a pixie, and I think I could beat Blossom in an arm wrestling match." Daniel replied.

Brock hit Daniel, hard. It hurt. But Daniel didn't let it show. He nodded, said, "Have a nice day." and turned to leave.

Brock punched the wall. It left a hole, and stormed off.

Daniel noticed that Irlore was sitting in a levitating chair watching them, and eating popcorn. "Why didn't you stop that?" Daniel asked.

"You seemed to have it under control." Irlore explained. He then tossed a piece of popcorn into the air, which exploded.

The girl ran up to Daniel, "Thanks for standing up for me. I'm Donna." She then looked at him closer. "You're going to have a black eye!"

Daniel shrugged. "Better me than you."

Chapter 9: The Capture

Daniel went toward his father's classroom a little before 9:00 that night. He wore his father's jacket and hat, hoping it would fool Brock. He breathed deeply, trying to calm himself down.

His phone vibrated. He picked it up and looked at it. A message from Velvet read, "Good Luck! We have your back."

He opened the door to the building cautiously. Surely Brock was going to jump him at any moment. He was right. Brock and his gang grabbed him and put a sack over his head. Daniel couldn't see where they were taking him, and hoped his friends could find him.

It seemed like a very long walk since he was being carried by ogres. When they finally put him down and took the bag off his head,

Brock jumped back. "Daniel?" he yelled. "You're not your dad. You don't tutor Latin."

"Non ego facio," Daniel replied, which in Latin means, *No, I don't.*

Brock, of course, did not understand. He and the other ogres tied Daniel to a chair with a rope.

"Not so tough now," Brock mocked. He pointed to the black eye he'd given Daniel and threatened, "What we'll do now is much worse than that."

He pulled his fist back to punch, but Sam interjected, "Stop! Just let him go. He's not worth it."

Brock thought for a moment then exclaimed, "He could be worth something. Sam, write a ransom note to his dad. I bet he'll pay big to get his son back."

"No," Sam refused. "I wrote the Latin note under protest. It was just stupid, but this is illegal. I don't do ransoms. I quit." Brock glared at him. "I know," Sam responded. "You'll feed me to the vegetarian dragon." He then walked out.

Profeser petter,
    we have captchered you're sun, give us monney and a A in you're klass to git him bak. you have until tommorow. NOT frum. Brock, Butch, Chad, Dave, and Drew

Translation:

Professor Peter,
    We have captured your son. Give us money and an A in your class to get him back. You have until tomorow.

Not from: Brock, Butch, Chad, Dave, and Drew

"It doesn't matter!" Brock fumed, yelling after him. "We don't need you. We can write a ransom note." He then stopped. "Does anyone here know how to spell?"

The other ogres gathered around and they all wrote the note. Daniel had fun telling them the wrong way to spell words when they asked him.

When the note was done, it read, "Profeser petter, we have captchered you're sun, give us monney and a A in you're klasss to git him bak. you have until tommorow. Not frum Brock, Butch, Chad, Dave, and Drew."

"My dad will be terrified by that," Daniel mocked. "He hates bad spelling and grammar." Then he suggested, "Do you want me to deliver the message to him? I know where he lives."

"Good ide..." Chad started to say, but Brock smacked him.

"You are so stupid!" Brock scolded. "He can't deliver a message. He's tied up." He turned to Dave. "Deliver this message to Daniel's dad."

"I don't know the address," Dave responded.

"I know it," Daniel told him. "It's #1 Dimwit Street."

"Where's that?" Chad asked.

Daniel tried to keep a straight face as he answered, "Just go south and tell someone you're looking for the #1 Dimwit. I'm sure he'll point out the answer for you."

Brock told Dave, "Go south, and ask for directions to the #1 Dimwit." He pointed at Chad. "You go with him." They left, that was good for Daniel, since that left three.

As soon as they left, Daniel laughed.

"What's so funny?" Brock yelled.

"Nothing," Daniel responded with a straight face.

They then heard a loud scream out in the courtyard. Brock and Butch ran out to see what was going on. Drew stayed to keep an eye on Daniel, but looked out the window to see if he could see what was going on.

Daniel whispered, "Clorma-ferno," and made a fireball in his hand that he used to burn through the ropes.

Drew turned around. "What's that smell? Is someone cooking dinner?"

Daniel got up, pulled a small spray bottle from his jacket pocket, and sprayed lemon juice in Drew's face.

As Drew put his hands to his face and complained, "That burns, and smells awful!" Daniel ran out of the room.

He saw Brock and Butch coming back, so he dove into another classroom and climbed out the window.

He met up with Velvet, Conner, and Blossom. "Good job with the distraction. It all went as planned."

Chapter 10: Fairy Cookies

It was several days later when Daniel, Velvet, and Conner were helping Blossom and the fairies clean up after their bake sale. Fairies were actually very good cooks, but Daniel's mother was right to warn him not to drink anything they gave him. The humans who accepted fairy punch all began uncontrollably singing and dancing. The

sprites ran around clucking like chickens. The trolls began slapping themselves. Of course, fairy punch had no effect on Rowan, which was disappointing, as the fairies wanted to see him sprout pink flowers.

It was getting very dark as they packed up. Brock came over and demanded of the fairies, "Give me all your cookies that are left, except the lemon cookies."

Daniel walked over to him. "Try asking nicely."

Brock puffed up his chest as if he were going to threaten Daniel, but then stepped

back. "Give me all your cookies, except the lemon, please?"

Blossom came over and handed him a bagful of pistachio cookies.

Brock glared at Daniel. "Watch your back! You won't get away again."

Daniel didn't reply because the fairies started screaming. He wondered why until he saw about ten zombies coming toward them. "What are those?" Daniel asked.

"Zombies," Velvet answered. "This is not normal."

The zombies all tried to attack Brock, moaning some sort of question as they advanced.

"Help him!" Daniel called to everyone. "Clorma-ferno!" he called, as he charged into the fight.

Velvet and Conner joined in too, but many of the fairies hid.

Brock was a good fighter, but he had a half dozen zombies on him. He knocked two out, but got knocked down by another. Two zombies held him down while a third was about to bite his throat, a deadly attack.

"Clorma-ferno!" Daniel called in a near panic. He not only created a fireball, but he threw one, blasting the zombie attacker. He then ran over and pulled one of the other zombies off of Brock, which made it so Brock could get up and get back in the fight.

They all fought hard and beat the zombies. When the fight was over, the zombies disintegrated into ash. Everyone else sat on the grass, stunned.

"What just happened?" Daniel asked.

"No idea," Velvet answered. "This shouldn't have happened. No spell can

summon zombies. I don't know a race who can either."

Brock moaned, "That hurt!"

They looked over and noticed that he was lying on the grass with his arm bleeding from the zombies sharp claws.

Daniel went over to help him, but when the fairies saw him, they came over and insisted that they take care of him.

As they did, Brock looked over at Daniel. "You saved my life."

"I'm not the enemy," Daniel responded. "It was the right thing to do."

Brock nodded. "Maybe not all humans are bad. You can stay."

He didn't say more because the fairies poured punch in his mouth to ease the pain.

Daniel hoped he was in good hands and sat back down by Velvet. "Why would zombies attack Brock?"

"I don't know," Velvet admitted. She looked over at Conner. "Do you know?"

"No idea," Conner answered. "I doubt ogres taste good."

Daniel looked contemplative. "I guess this is just the beginning of our adventures together at this school."

Velvet assured him, "No matter what we face, ogres, zombies, or anything else, as long as we stick together we'll be fine."

The touching moment was broken by Brock, who had too much fairy punch, jumping up and screaming, "I want some lemons!!!"

The End

of Book 1, but the adventure is just beginning.

Look for more books in the series!

About the Author

Michael Greene is a 13 year old, who loves science, theater, and coming up with cool characters and stories. He also enjoys spinning a fire staff, and is working on getting his eagle scout.

He has been part of the writing team at DeBokton Book for the past two years, helping develop characters for stories. He came up with Fangs, Derek, and Tim in the Eubos System books and with the entire city of Alfir in the FaeBorn series.

Michael is known for his quirky sense of humor. This is his first fantasy book. Look for more coming in the series.

Look for more books in this series and other great books at

dlb

DeBokton Book

DeBokton.weebly.com

Proof

Made in the USA
Columbia, SC
05 March 2018